USBORNE FIRST
Level On...

USBORNE FIRST READING

The Three Wishes

Retold by Lesley Sims
Illustrated by Elisa Squillace

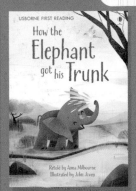

USBORNE FIRST READING

How the Elephant got his Trunk

Retold by Anna Milbourne
Illustrated by John Joven

USBORNE FIRST READING

How the Whale got his Throat

Retold by Anna Milbourne
Illustrated by John Joven

Usborne First Reading

King Midas and the Gold

Retold by Alex Frith
Illustrated by Simona Sanfilippo

USBORNE FIRST READING

How the Rhino got his Skin

Retold by Rosie Dickins
Illustrated by John Joven

USBORNE FIRST READING

The Ant and the Grasshopper

Retold by Katie Daynes
Illustrated by Marci Rosenblum

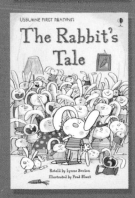

USBORNE FIRST READING

The Rabbit's Tale

Retold by Lynne Benton
Illustrated by Fred Blunt

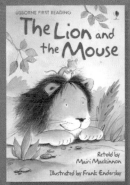

USBORNE FIRST READING

The Lion and the Mouse

Retold by Mairi Mackinnon
Illustrated by Frank Endersby

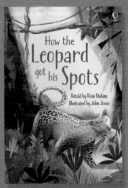

USBORNE FIRST READING

How the Leopard got his Spots

Retold by Rosie Dickins
Illustrated by John Joven

Why the Kangaroo Jumps

by Rudyard Kipling

Retold by Rob Lloyd Jones

Illustrated by John Joven

Reading consultant: Alison Kelly

Long ago, the first kangaroo was short and stumpy.

He yelled at the gods,
"Make me different!"

Kangaroo kept yelling.

The gods called
to a wild dog.

Make
Kangaroo
different.

The dog grinned.

Then it charged
at Kangaroo.

The dog chased
Kangaroo across the
dry, dusty desert.

He chased him between
towering mountains...

...and through long grass and short grass.

Kangaroo came
to a river.

Kangaroo rose
onto his back legs –
and jumped!

He jumped across
the river.

Kangaroo kept
on jumping.

His back legs grew
stronger. His tail
grew longer.

He jumped back
to where he began.

"Why did that dog chase me?" he yelled.

"You wanted to be different," a god replied.

Kangaroo sighed.
Then he jumped away.

And that is why
kangaroos jump today.

PUZZLES

Puzzle 1

Put the pictures in order.

A

B

C

D

Puzzle 2

Match the words
to the pictures.

dog   snake   god

kangaroo   river

Puzzle 3
Choose the correct word for each picture.

jumped river grinned

The dog
_____.

He came to
a _____.

Kangaroo
_____.

Puzzle 4
Spot five differences between the two pictures.

Answers to puzzles

Puzzle 1

1D

2C

3B

4A

Puzzle 2

snake

kangaroo

river

dog

god

Puzzle 3

The dog <u>grinned</u>.

He came to a <u>river</u>.

Kangaroo <u>jumped</u>.

Puzzle 4

About the story

This story is from the book *Just So Stories* by Rudyard Kipling, which tells how animals came to be the way they are.

Designed by Laura Nelson
Cover design by Sam Whibley
Series designer: Russell Punter
Series editor: Lesley Sims

First published in 2017 by Usborne Publishing Ltd., Usborne House, 83-85 Saffron Hill, London EC1N 8RT, England. www.usborne.com

32